# Sam, Elli, and the Bully Sharks

**Mrs. Pebbles & The OES Young Authors Guild**
Illustrated by Aimee Falat

Dedicated to our families and our OES family, who inspire us to do great things!

**Edited by** Mrs. Brenda Jicha and Ms. Debby Stuebs

## The OES Young Authors Guild

Harper Burke
Willow Burke
Elli Gaffney
Maycee Heimke
Reese Kryger
Collin Kurz
Reese Miller
Paige Radzinski
Maria Suarez

Way out in the sea, far from land, is where I call my home. My name is Sam. My skin is smooth and grey and I love to swim.

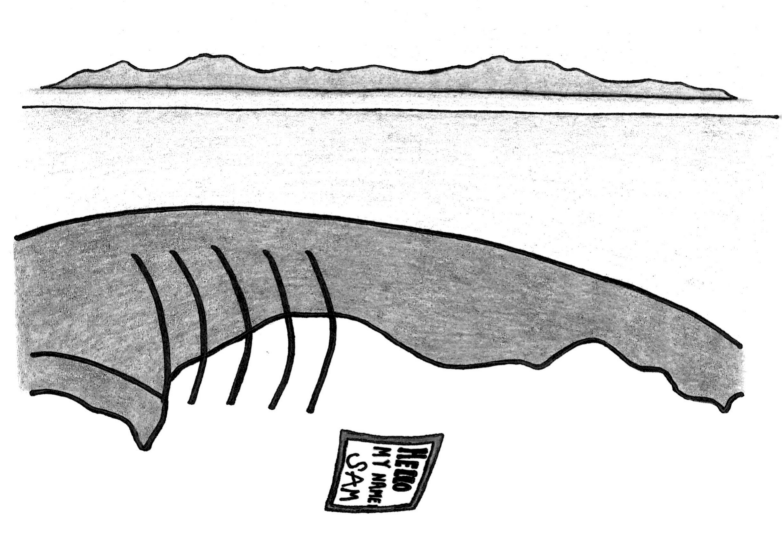

Don't be afraid when I smile at you. My nose is big and my teeth are even bigger. Please don't swim away when you see my smiling face.

Each time I try to make a new friend, it doesn't work out. They see me and swim away as fast as they can. I'm afraid they don't like what they see. I don't fit in.

Sometimes, I care too much about what others think of me, so I try to be like them.

I am not a narwhal, but I tried to be.

I am not a blowfish, but I tried to be.

I am not a turtle, but I tried to be.

In the end, I decided to like me and I do, most of the time.

I am a SHARK!  A vegetarian shark.  I love seaweed!

Trying to find a friend takes a lot of work. Sometimes I get sad because I think it should be easier, but it's not.

I tried to hide from those who treat me badly, but that doesn't work.

I treated them just as bad as they treated me because I was hurt. That did not feel good.

I asked them to STOP! I have explained to them how their unkind words made me feel, but they didn't listen.

I decided to treat them like I wish they would treat me. That feels right. It takes perseverance and a positive attitude.

Even though I struggle with making friends, I am thankful for what I have. Each morning I swim out to greet the sun, the rolling waves, the morning colors, and the sound of gulls overhead. There is always something to be thankful for. I am thankful for this place I call home.

Bull and Lee are two sharks that treat me badly. They think I should eat like them and they say my teeth are weird and my nose is big. They don't say nice things.

"Hey Sam! Sharks eat what they meet in the sea. You are a strange shark!"

"Nice to see you guys. I saw a whole swarm of krill in the coral reef. They just laughed.

"What a weirdo," they said.

I was not going to let them ruin my day.

I decided to go for a morning swim, and as I swam I heard something barking low and sad.

I followed the sound far out to sea where the waters carry big chunks of ice. As I swam, the cries became louder.

When I got closer, I peeked out of the water and saw a fuzzy, white seal pup on a large slab of ice. I decided to circle-in to see if I could help. She was all alone out on the ice. I poked my head closer and said, "What's wrong? Why are you crying?"

She looked at me with tear filled eyes.

"I am all alone out here and I can't find my way home," She cried.

"What's your name?" I asked.

"Elli," she sighed.

"Hi Elli. My name is Sam. Come in the water Elli, and I will help you find your way home."

"You're a SHARK!" said Elli. "I don't want you to eat me!"

"I am a vegetarian," said Sam.

Elli looked at Sam and chuckled. "Ha-ha. I've never heard that before. Go away!" said Elli.

Sam started to swim away, but Bull and Lee popped their heads out of the water.

"We're vegetarians too, Elli. Jump in the water so we can have breakfast."

"Go away," said Elli.

Bull and Lee would not leave her alone. They started to rock the chunk of ice Elli was on. Elli looked scared.

"Leave her alone!" said Sam.

"Why should we?" growled Bull and Lee.

"Elli has a family looking for her and they might be here any minute," said Sam.

Bull and Lee nervously looked around. Seal mothers and fathers could be very fierce.

Sam gently nudged the ice chunk Elli was on and pushed her farther out to sea. Elli was quiet. When it looked like they were alone Elli said, "Thank you Sam."

Each day Sam continued to push the ice chunk closer to where Elli believed her family was, but with each passing day, the ice chunk Elli was on began to melt.

Bull and Lee were never far away.

"You two are so strange," they yelled.

"Sam, stop playing with OUR dinner!" laughed Bull and Lee.

Then one day in the distance, we could hear the bellowing of the seal colony.

"There," said Elli, "I see home!"
Sam looked over and saw an icy mountain.
At the top, the Seal King sat looking out to sea with the rest of the colony speckled all around on the icy cliffs.

Elli started to bark and pound the ice.
The seal colony began to roar. Elli was home.
Sam smiled. "We're almost there Elli."

In all the excitement, no one saw the boat nearby had dropped a large net. Bull and Lee were caught in the net!

Without hesitation, Sam dove to rescue them. All Sam could do was to tear a small hole in the net with his big teeth. The hole was too small for Bull and Lee to get out of, but not for Elli.

Before she plunged into the icy water, Elli called her family for help. She jumped into the water along with her father and the colony of seals. They were not going to lose Elli again!

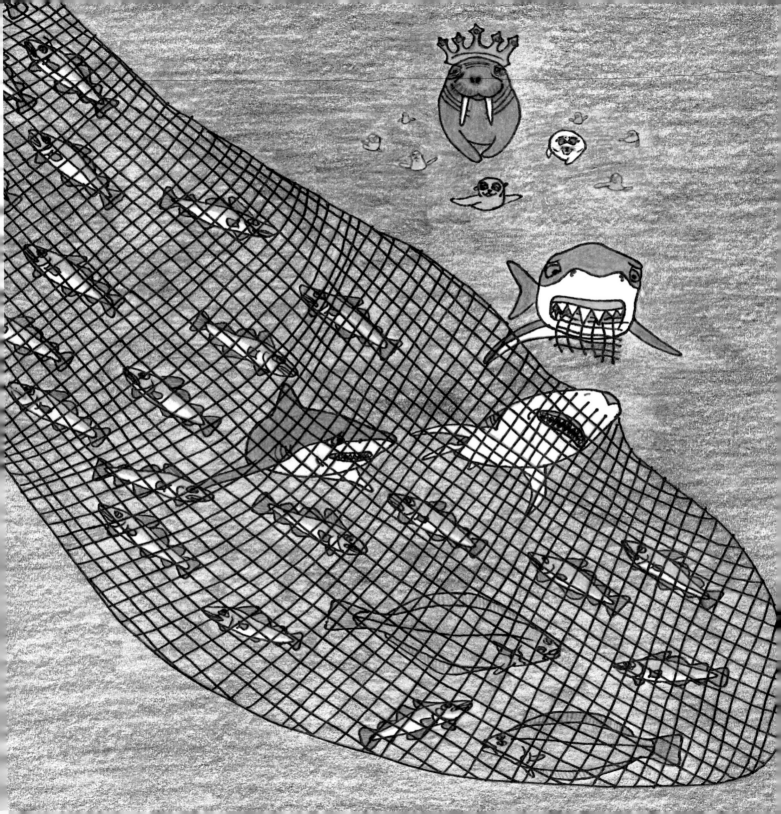

Elli swam into the small hole in the net and headed straight to the top, hoping to release the net from the large hook that dangled just under the water's surface.

The Seal King, Sam, and the colony lifted the net up so Elli could unhook it. The net dropped, freeing Bull and Lee. They were saved!

Bull and Lee could not believe that Sam and Elli and the seal colony had saved them.

The great Seal King swam closer to Bull and Lee.

"Please forgive us, we have not been kind," said Bull and Lee.

"Yes, the great sea tells of your unkind ways, but today is a new beginning." said the Seal King. "From this day forward you must learn from your mistakes, be wise, treat others kindly, and help others when you can."

"We will," said Bull and Lee. "We promise, but we are afraid.  We have not been kind to others. What if they do not forgive us?"

"They will," said the Seal King.

The Seal King thrust his long tusks into the water setting the sea in motion and commanded: "Let your new ways roll forth as the waters flow in the great sea, may your kindness flow like the sea and never dry up."

The Seal King looked tenderly at Sam and said, "The great sea tells of your ways, too, Sam. You are a GREAT White Shark and you are magnificent!" Sam smiled.

"My daughter has returned home with the help of an unlikely friend, but a friend all the same. "Thank you Sam," said the seal king.

Elli swam to shore with her family. When she reached the cliffs, she looked back to see Sam smiling. Elli smiled back. They were friends.

# What we learned

- Don't be too worried about what others think of you.
- Don't try to be something you are not.
- Be proud of who you are.
- Never give up.
- Stay positive.
- Be thankful.
- Communicate.
- Don't be afraid to ask for help.
- Learn from your mistakes.
- Be a friend.
- Treat others the way you want to be treated.

Made in the USA
Lexington, KY
02 April 2018